Amanda's
DINOSAUR

by Wendy Orr
illustrated by Gillian Campbell

ISBN 0-590-42443-2

Text copyright © 1988 by Wendy Orr.

Illustrations copyright © 1988 by Gillian Campbell.

All rights reserved. Published by Scholastic Inc.,
730 Broadway, New York, NY 10003, by arrangement with
Ashton Scholastic Pty Limited.

12 11 10 9 8 7 6 5 4 3 2 1   0 1 2 3 4/9

Printed in the U.S.A.   08

First Scholastic printing, October 1990

SCHOLASTIC INC.
New York Toronto London Auckland Sydney

Amanda and her mother and father lived on a farm with:

cows and dogs, rabbits and cats
   kangaroos and possums, wallabies and wombats
     parrots and chickens, peacocks and emus
      turtles and snakes, and lizards.

But Amanda wanted a dinosaur.

It was spring.
There were baby animals everywhere.

Babies that had hatched and lived by themselves.
Babies feeding from their mothers.
Babies in pouches.
Babies in eggs.

"How would a baby dinosaur be born?" asked Amanda.

"Probably from an egg," answered her mother.

Amanda's mother was planting a tree for the possums.
Deep in the earth she found an old hollow log.
So she dug it out for the rabbits to play in.

Amanda watched the rabbits.
  They ran in one end
    ...and out they came.
      They ran in the other end
        ...and out they came.

They could not run through the fattest part of the log!
Amanda looked inside.

Amanda's mother was collecting eggs from the hen house.

"How big is a dinosaur's egg?" asked Amanda.

"Bigger than an emu's egg," said her mother.
"Why, have you found one?"

"Yes," said Amanda.

Amanda put her arm down the log.
The egg was cold and hard and a bit bumpy,
not smooth like a hen's egg.

She tried to wiggle it out of the log,
but it did not move.

She tried to shake it out of the log,
but it did not move.

Amanda's mother was talking to the parrots.

"How does a dinosaur get out of its egg?" asked Amanda.

"I suppose by pecking, like a bird," said her mother.

"How do they know when it's time to start pecking?"

"They just know," said her mother.

Amanda went back to her log.
She put her hand in to touch the egg again.
It was still cold and hard and rough.

She was just about to take her hand away,
when she felt something else.
A tap-tap-tapping came from deep inside the egg.
Amanda tried with her other hand.
The tap-tap-tapping grew stronger.

The egg cracked.
Amanda watched.
The crack got bigger.
Soon she could see the hard top of a little snout.

The little snout tap-tap-tapped some more.
Then there was a little green head
and a long thin neck
and a little fat body
with four short legs
and a long wrinkled tail.

The baby dinosaur crawled out and looked at Amanda.

Amanda looked back at the dinosaur.

"Are you hungry?" she asked him.

The dinosaur didn't answer.

She gave him some hay.
But he didn't eat it.
She gave him a carrot.
But he didn't eat that.

Amanda's mother was feeding the calves.

"What does a baby dinosaur eat?" Amanda asked.

"Probably fresh grass," said her mother.
"Or soft plants like lettuce. Maybe a little milk."

Amanda gave her dinosaur a bowl of milk.
He lapped it all up and looked at Amanda.

Amanda gave him some nice juicy lettuce.
He ate it all up and looked at Amanda.

Amanda gave him armfuls of fresh green grass.
He ate it all up and then he was happy.

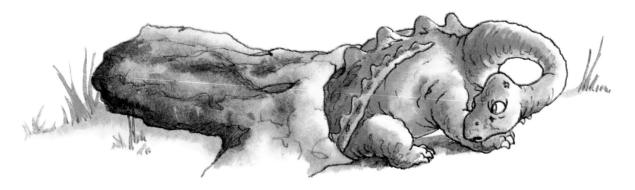

Amanda's dinosaur grew very fast.
Soon he was too big for his log.

Soon he was enormous!

It was nearly dark.

Amanda's mother had gone to get hay for the cows.

Everything was quiet and sleepy.
Amanda was nearly asleep.

Suddenly...
...she saw a fox sneaking around the hen house.
Amanda was frightened!

She saw a fox sneaking around the rabbit hutch.
Amanda was mad!

Amanda whistled for her dinosaur.

"Lie down," she said, and climbed on his back.

Around and around the garden
the fox chased the chickens and the rabbits.

Around and around the garden
Amanda's dinosaur chased the fox.

Cows mooed, dogs barked,
  cats meowed, rabbits hopped,
    kangaroos bounced, wombats waddled,
      chickens clucked, parrots screeched,
        lizards scurried, snakes hissed.

Amanda shouted and her dinosaur roared.

Amanda and her dinosaur chased the fox
down the path and out the gate
down the drive and out to the road.

Amanda's mother came running back.
She looked at the garden.
Flowers were trampled, branches were broken.
White feathers were scattered with bits of red fur.

"What on earth happened?" she asked.

"I don't think dinosaurs like foxes," said Amanda.